THE GREAT CRIME

FREDERICK S. GOLD

First Edition

PAGE PUBLISHING
Conneaut Lake, PA

First originally published by Page Publishing 2023

ISBN 979-8-88960-808-0 (pbk)
ISBN 979-8-88960-821-9 (digital)

Printed in the United States of America

For Barbara With Love

CONTENTS

PROLOGUE

It was four in the morning, and the moon was three-fourths full. It was very quiet. Marion Alright, Hassad Orvitz, and Bannita Wassit were somewhat relaxed after committing what was to become perhaps the most horrific crime of all time. Alright was driving, very cautiously, and each one had a hand resting comfortably on the trigger. They were prepared to be quiet, cautious, and low profile, and they had practiced a hundred times how to behave if they were stopped. If they were asked to get out of the car—an unlikely event—the officer or officers would be dead in an instant. It would be good to avoid that. It would have to be hidden until the morning, at which time it wouldn't matter. The thought forced a wry smile—but made no sound—from each of them.

Alright stayed under the speed limit, and the other two were apparently dozing but alert. Alright was a white man, an unimaginable help, and seemed quiet, almost sheepish, beneath his cold-blooded manner. Orvitz was a Muslim, and the three had ad nauseam discussed how to use it. Wassit was a happy-go-lucky killer, who seemed not to be bothered by it at all, and the third mastermind being a woman—and a good-looking one at that—gave them special cover and an uncommon advantage.

They were headed en route by the Taconic to Poughkeepsie. There, one of them would pay cash and get on a train to Rochester. One of them would take a bus to Pittsburgh. And one would continue to drive until Cincinnati, park the car, and disappear, or rather, until he would be called again. They were each very good, and they knew they would have to be. Bannita Wassit had killed many times before, but never like this, and always covert. Their proudest fact was the way they had used no one else whom they knew—except one person—to hatch their plot, and they actually felt a little sad that they probably would never be known.

As the night began to wane, they prepared for their departure. Orvitz got out of the car, said a half-hearted goodbye, and went off to the train station with his small bag. They had practiced a million times so that their car stayed out of the station's camera range. Alright and Wassit eased into the local Greyhound station, where he and Wassit repeated the maneuver. Alright would be the only one who would hear the unimaginable events on the radio—at about ten that morning—and he would have no one to share it with. He would act out sharing the dread at a gas station just off the highway a few minutes later. Then it would be done; all the thought and planning and all hell would break loose.

THE CRIME

Andy Bassoon awoke at 6:00. He glanced at his wife, who was still asleep, and slowly got up while still yawning. He was thirty-seven; had a son, aged nine, and a daughter, aged six; and somehow managed to say thank you to his lucky stars each morning.

His wife was beautiful, a brunette, bubbly and bright, and about the best thing he could think of in the world. Andy was a rising star in the FBI. He was quick and funny, and everyone liked him. He was on the fast track, loved the service, had a purple star from Afghanistan, and had his BA from Fordham. He had just moved into a small house right over the line in Pelham.

He took a shower, got dressed, walked into the kitchen, and sat down for breakfast. His wife, Maria, gave him a kiss and poured him some coffee. He heard the children begin their ritual, and he smiled at the thought. His six-year-old daughter rushed out and jumped onto his lap, giggling the whole way. He knew that she would have to get dressed soon and get ready for kindergarten, which was a thought he loved, and he loved the fact that Maria would drive her to school. His nine-year-old came out looking grumpy, grumbled something he couldn't understand, and popped out a piece of toast right from the toaster. He looked around, said he couldn't do something, and grumbled another something when his mother told him where it was. He smiled when his son went up to get dressed.

He finished his breakfast and prepared to leave. It was about 7:15, and he was now fully awake. He took his wife in his arms, gave her a long kiss, said that he loved her, and walked out the front door.

He felt the autumn chill in the air, started up the car, and eased out onto the road.

The phone rang. "Bassoon," he said. The caller said something that sounded like gibberish, the way that agents sounded; he responded in kind, and he continued calmly on his way.

At just about 8:15, he rolled into the parking garage, got out of the car, and headed for work. As he got into the elevator, his friend Ralph gave him a tap on the shoulder, and he said, "How ya doing, sport?"

Ralph said, "Never better," and they opened up the FBI wing.

Andy slid into his cubicle, where he found two urgent calls. Both were from superiors, and he half expected them. They both related to the morning's events, and he grunted as he learned that he would be activated for the president after all. So he called an acknowledgment and headed right for the UN. He knew traffic would be a nightmare, but he had his badge and was ready for anything.

He parked about six blocks from the UN, called his superior, and started walking quickly toward his location. It was just before 9:00.

It was a hellish nightmare. Everyone was talking loudly, was going somewhere, and seemed distracted. His superior smiled upon seeing him, shook his hand, said something funny, and laid out his plan. He would be walking in the back behind the president, looking for anything out of the ordinary, and telling his superior if he saw anything unusual. His microphone had a special call button, which was connected directly to the entire secret service detail, in case he needed an urgent message. He smiled at the care with which it had been planned out. What a country.

He saw two FBI comrades whom he knew and gave them friendly waves. No time now for friendly chatter. He had about an hour till the president took the stage, and all his instincts, not to mention his FBI training, were activated.

He covered every inch of his territory and looked at it again. He covered it twice. He walked slightly into the adjoining grid and smiled at the FBI agent. He covered it a third time. It was getting crowded. He stepped back and looked at the big picture, and it all seemed good. They had no reports of anything.

Finally, he heard the president's motorcade, and it seemed somewhat confident. He saw the three special service details he knew, and they looked tense and ready for anything, as they should be. The president quickly entered the back door, disappeared, until he came into full view of the audience, and seemed transformed into his full-fledged public persona. His brief report to his superiors was all good.

The person who took the stand came out, waved politely, and proceeded to introduce the president. Truth was, it was really just a formal exercise to be used as practice for the big event next month, but the crowd loved it and cheered wildly. The podium, its care and security, was the responsibility of one of the best security men in the FBI, along with the best detail the secret service could muster. Bassoon looked at each of them, and he was happy with the result.

The president came out and seemed happy. Precious few knew he only had seconds to live. He walked to the microphone and said, "My fellow Americans," and a terrible bleeping sound came out, followed by an immense explosion. It enveloped him. He was dead in an instant, along with a secret service agent and the man who had introduced him. Then all hell broke loose. The secret service and FBI were instantly in charge, not that it mattered. It was clear that the president was dead in a blink of an eye, and, in the midst of the carnage, everyone was stunned. Everyone looked for someone who caused it, but there was no one. There was pandemonium in the crowd; people screamed and ran, and finally, after a few seconds that seemed like an eternity, the television anchors said, "Oh my god, the president is dead, the president is dead!"

Bassoon tried to find something in the crowd, but to no avail. All his instincts kicked in, and they were substantial. The crowd was shocked, and people were screaming, yelling, and crying. He could not see a single person who looked out of place. He called the radio and heard his superiors screaming, trying to find out what happened, but even they were dumbfounded and clueless. He tried to give help to the wounded, but they were all being attended to, and then he saw the president's body. It was terrible. His face had been virtually blown off, and his secret service kept him from the television crews, who were trying to get a glimpse, with very little results. For a fleeting second, he recalled the scenes of President Kennedy, which he had watched many times since he had not been born yet.

The television shows were all interrupted, and whoever was available to be on the air looked dazed and had precious little to say except that the president was dead. No one seemed to know anything. The many networks could learn nothing from their ground crews, who were frantically trying to learn something, anything. The chaos was real.

Some relatively calm, backup men tried to ask people where the vice president was, but it was several minutes before anyone could get an answer. It turned out that Anne Jennings, a mid-level reporter at one of the television stations, was with him for an interview, and her superiors frantically tried to get her on the screen. They finally were able to do that, with her feed logged on to all stations, large and small, including radio, when she looked harried and said, "The vice president is being protected and will be sworn in as president today. He is being moved to Camp David as we speak. He is not yet available for any comments until authorities determine if he is in any danger. Stay tuned for further developments."

That was all she could get at the moment, and her superiors were relieved. But the thoughts kept coming. Wait a minute. If they were taking him to Camp David, would they really say so, and did they know something that we didn't? Would they take him to the air when there was no reason to fly, and would they say what they definitively decided to do? A quick parlay among senior executives led to the tentative conclusion that they would take him to the bunker inside the White House, and they couldn't get anyone to confirm or deny.

It was a frantic search for answers, but since none seemed coming, even tentatively, Bassoon seemed more and more uneasy. Something was wrong. He called his superiors and shared his fear. They didn't know what to say. There was precious little left of the bomb, which had been blown to bits, but his superiors asked him—no, directed him—to gather whatever could be found and to label the scene an accident and reserved for FBI activity. This was done, and it gave Bassoon precious little comfort. It seemed that the FBI suddenly had dozens of agents on the scene.

He moved to a private space and asked to speak to Evans Waters. Waters was assistant director of the FBI, a superior and a man of impeccable taste, three tours in Iraq, fifty-two, and someone Bassoon could trust with his life. He was primarily responsible for Bassoon's rise through the FBI's ranks. He sounded unusually calm and listened intently. When he was through, Bassoon waited for what seemed like an eternity and then heard, "Come in. I'll leave a pass for you and come right through."

It seemed like an eternity before Bassoon got back to the office. He parked ran to the elevator and went right to Waters's floor. Two very mean-looking men stood right by the door, asked who he was, gave him his pass, and told him where to go. It was the large conference room in the executive suite. It was chaos. Everyone seemed to be yelling. He looked around, found Waters, and walked right toward him. Waters grabbed him by the neck, took him into the little room next door, slammed the door, and asked to tell him the whole story. He did, slowly, and left nothing out. Waters was silent for a long minute. He then spoke,

"Bassoon, there is something wrong. We don't know anything. We had no prior chatter, no warning of any kind, we have no suspects, and there must be a story. What set the bomb off? How was it timed? It blew to smithereens, so we don't know a thing about it. The bomb squad is trying to gain something, but even they are dumbfounded."

"I knew very quickly that we were caught flat-footed. Totally surprised. And trust me, there was no one, unless he was very good, who could have set that bomb off with a timer," said Bassoon.

"You saw so one?" said Waters.

"I saw no one who looked suspicious. I was right there. There was no one who acted remotely suspicious. It was stunning," said Bassoon.

"There had to be something. Was it loaded into the speaker? It had to be. Was it timed to go off? It couldn't have been because it was triggered when he said, 'My fellow Americans.' That wasn't timed. How did they do it? It must have been timed to those words, or someone set if off. There is no other choice. But unless we find out which, we are in deep shit. There is no way to know if there is another," said Waters.

Waters's last words were terrifying. He was right. They would have to do something.

Bassoon talked very slowly now. He was thinking as he went along. "Waters, do we have to figure it out before the vice president is sworn in?"

"You bet we do. Or else we don't know if it is safe."

Bassoon was dumbfounded, but he knew Waters was right.

"Jesus," he said.

They both allowed some time to pass. Then Waters said, "Andy, you have to get to Washington. See what they are doing with the vice president. Stay in touch the whole time, and try to find out what you can on the phone. Talk to me every few minutes. We have the head of the FBI's plane here. I'll get you clearance. I'll also call the assistant head of the FBI and tell him what's happening. You have to tell me what they are going to do with the vice president. By the way, I'll call your wife. Go with God, but go fast."

"I was thinking of the same thing. I'll be there as fast as I can," said Bassoon.

Bassoon was in a car, with lights and sirens to LaGuardia, and on the FBI plane in no time. It didn't have to wait. The ride would be about forty-five minutes to Washington, and then he'd have a car there. He learned on the plane that the vice president was in the White House bunker, was okay, and that he would soon make some assurance to the American people. Whether he would be sworn in or not was hotly being disputed. The president's family was being taken care of, and he could only imagine the horror that they were going through. He tried to share some advice on the plane that they hold off swearing in the vice president, but he was too junior to be listened to, and the senior-most men would ultimately make that decision.

He doubled his urgency. He sped to the White House; gave the security men, armed with tactical weapons, his top-level security; ran through the place; stopped at the thorough, top security all around; and was finally—but slowly methodically—brought down through the most solid security in the world. His entrance into this hallowed group caused no interruption whatsoever. He had learned that they decided to swear in the vice president, show it on television with a slight delay, and keep the vice president safe the whole time. His first act was to be a declaration of mourning and then to tend to the president's family.

As he entered, he looked around, and it looked well enough under control. Almost no one was present, except the vice president and an associate justice of the Supreme Court. No one else. The associate justice of the Supreme Court spoke.

"Ladies and gentlemen," he said.

And the vice president repeated, "My fellow Americans."

A terrible bleeping sound came out, followed by an immense explosion. Just like that, the vice president was dead. The television was canceled just right after the explosion, and the vice president's face as well as the associate justice of the Supreme Court was shown blowing up the screen.

Bassoon merely looked in horror.

The FBI agents who were there—precious few, mind you—looked hopelessly lost and were no good to anyone. They were mostly trying to give aid to the vice president and the associate justice of the Supreme Court, but there was nothing any of them could do. Bassoon realized that he had been the only one let in, and the only one there who had seen both bombs. He called Waters again on the line, and Waters was giving orders.

"Don't let anyone touch the bomb. We have to preserve it," he said. "Bassoon, you get goddamn pictures of everything. Have everyone give their name to my FBI agent, and get everyone else the hell out of there."

Bassoon took all the pictures he could. They were all silently thinking about how they would be used, and they did not like the prospect. The senior folks who had made the decision not to wait were beside themselves, and even they had severe palpitations. And they were looking at the poor vice president and the associate justice of the Court, and they were dumbfounded. Some of the senior staffers of the secret service and the FBI were crying.

Bassoon finished his assignment, quickly gave orders, said from where, and called Waters again.

Waters said, "Listen, Bassoon, here's what we're going to do. I've ordered a team to take over the White House. Download all your pictures, give them to the team, keep copies, and bring them to FBI headquarters. I'll meet you there. We'll set up a task force. I'm already moving. We've got the speaker of the House, keeping her safe and quiet, will not let her speak to anyone, and will not tell anyone where. We won't swear her in until I'm good and ready. There's something going on, and we have to learn what it is. The director is going to speak to the nation."

Bassoon followed his orders to a tee and frankly, said very little to anyone. His mind was racing a mile a minute. He insisted that he take all sorts of pictures of the place of the bomb and kept thinking wildly about how it had been set off. There was nothing left to see; it had been blown apart so intelligently, but he was sure the best people in the world, with two bombs to compare, could find something. He did realize that the associate justice of the Supreme Court had stupidly repeated, "My fellow Americans," and that the vice president had repeated them, but he felt surely that it was impossible to base a bomb on those precise words from a personal touch. He again looked around at the small number of people who had been in attendance, including the television crews, and knew that each person would be grilled mercilessly. The answer was no doubt in how the bomb had been made, how it had been hidden so effectively, and how the hell it had been set off at that precise time. He shuddered.

Two hours later, he was sitting in a chair at FBI headquarters, with what seemed like dozens of people around him. They were not talking.

At about 10:04 that morning, Marion had been listening to some local radio station. He smiled at the confusion. He listened intently, knew every step before it had happened, and was obscenely calm. He heard that the president was dead, heard the report from Anne Jennings, and knew everything being done in Washington. He knew the sequence that Bassoon was going through, knew Bassoon's name, and virtually knew every critical step that followed. He decided to wait a while before stopping at a rest stop just to be sure before he gave any pictures. He drove in the right-hand lane, at the speed limit, and looked carefully for any state speed limits. Under no circumstances did he make any contact with Orvitz or Wassit.

Finally, at about 11:30, he stopped for his first gas and restroom break. He paid cash for his gasoline, made some small talk with a lady and man while waiting for it to fill up, saw no one in the bathroom, and went on his way. At around 3:00, he pulled in to his prearranged place, an apartment in a middle-class location in Cincinnati, had a beer, and turned on the television. He saw the shock and reaction to the carnage in Washington.

Hassid Orvitz and Benita Wassit each arrived in Rochester and Pittsburgh at around the same time, and each similarly disappeared, by delving into the melting pot of the cities. They were each well-trained to keep to themselves.

Half a world away, there was a quiet smile in the KGB. It only affected a few people, and nothing was said. Those people were not known to Alright, who only knew they existed. He knew that, if something went wrong, he would be expected to die. Instant reward. He was well aware that he was expected to lie low, and he knew that his life depended on it.

This was the hardest part of his role, and he was well prepared for it. He already had food for a few days, clothes, and everything he needed. He relaxed and waited to see the third part of the plot. He knew that it would be the hardest.

As Bassoon sat and waited, his thoughts slowed down. It had only been about five hours since it all started, and it seemed like a lifetime had passed. He had not even talked to his wife, and he felt a knot in his stomach. He did not dare to call her now.

Waters walked in. He was ashen and talked very slowly.

"We don't have a president or vice president. It is simply unbelievable. Everyone here has been vetted as carefully as possible, and this room is the first place I will go. So let's get down to business," he said.

He repeated very slowly what had happened, and he used no names. He wanted no one involved. He stopped at the time of each explosion and emphasized that no one knew how the bomb had been established or set off. It was stunning. The two explosions were being pieced together, and it would take some time to recreate what happened. In the meantime, it was urgent that a plan be implemented and followed. There would be a third effort to swear in a president—probably tomorrow—and it would be conducted with the most care any nation could provide. It would probably not be televised.

He established three teams: one for each bombing and one to connect the two. Each team had a leader—kept secret—and the information gained would be widely disseminated among the three groups. No one would be permitted to disseminate any information to the press—even on deep background—without the express consent of the highest authorities. He would be in charge of coordinating the operation. Protection for the speaker of the House would be outside the group.

His words had a calming effect. Everyone's pulse dropped several points. He said that each assignment would be told to each person, and the three teams would then meet in three large rooms to being their work. Godspeed.

Bassoon was assigned to group three, the one to investigate the connection between the bombings. He talked directly to the group's supervisor, Randall Owens, whom he knew slightly, who was an eighteen-year man who kept his head down and did everything by the book. He knew Bassoon was the only man who had seen both bombs, and he hoped something could be jogged loose. So Bassoon was kept close, and every little thing was analyzed. The bombs are identical; they had been specially made; they were undecipherable by the most stringent standards used by the States; and they were tucked way under the podium used by the secret service, so it was almost impossible to see it. But there it was. The thing was, there was no way to know if there were any more. For all the FBI knew, there could be more waiting to go off, and they might be sitting idle for who knows how long.

So Bassoon focused on what was knowable. How in the world were bombs inserted in the secret service podia, and who put them there? He had to go back to when the podia had been manufactured and every step they had gone through since then. It was drudgery. It occurred to him that the bombs' maker must have known that and was counting on it. That thought was kept alive in his head, and there was perhaps a way to use it. Every thought he had was confirmed for his team.

A special team had been set up to find the bombs, and they finally found what they had been looking for. It was a doohickey way behind the underside of the podium, and the bomb-sniffing device of the secret service finally set it off. But it was not visible and not susceptible to the secret service's device unless the podium was turned just so. It was ingenious.

The particular podia were standard issue and had been ordered and made by a standard maker. Every single podium ordered for the United States was requested, and many had been made and ordered over recent time. The first ones ordered by New York and Washington were identified and collected. Turned out, there were many, but thank God, none had bombs hidden in them. It actually took days to check all the podia, and the work continued round the clock.

As the first night came to a close and as he was given a room to sleep in, he called his wife. She was hysterical but was easily calmed down. She knew he had been all right and was not surprised he had been called to Washington, but was just glad to hear his voice. He talked to each of his kids—school had been canceled till they knew everything was okay and everything seemed under control. He was able to tell them little about what he was doing, which they understood. They would feel better if they had a president and vice president. So he hunkered down and went to work.

It was hotly disputed how they would make the speaker of the House the president. The fear everyone had was palpable. Condolences came in from every corner of the globe, and they were answered by the State Department.

Finally, it was announced: She would be sworn in secretly and announced publicly afterward. Little did the public know that it was all a ruse.

It was Waters's idea. The set up was a trap. An FBI person was ostensibly to be sworn in and the oath administered by another FBI person. When and where it was to be was to be announced shortly before. There would be no podium used and under no circumstances, would anyone say, "My fellow Americans." If it all went as planned, the real speaker of the House—kept safely away—would be sworn in next by the actual chief justice of the Supreme Court.

The next day dawned with eager anticipation, and all the television talking heads were going full tilt. Almost all work had been canceled—except the urgent kind—and all hands were glued to the television. What was told was that the speaker of the House was being sworn in, in secret, and it would be announced when it was done, and the new president would then address the nation. No one was given a time, but it was widely assumed it would be in the afternoon.

In a two-bedroom apartment near the White House, the fourth member of the kill squad had been calmly waiting. He was part of one of the most capable squads in the world, kept to himself, and was being paid so much that he would never have to risk being on another job. The other three members of the kill squad only knew him by "Nell," a name they did not think was his. They had only met him once to be sure in case something happened, and even they had been impressed by his talents and his cold-blooded manner. He was middle-aged, some mix of brown; had a weird birthmark under his left arm; and was naturally very quiet. The thought of him made one shudder.

He had been in the apartment for weeks. The second bedroom had been walled off and was only accessible with a master code. It had been meticulously planned. In it, Nell could control all kinds of mayhem for miles around, but none was used, and none was intended, except one thing. He could see everything for seventy-five miles, in every direction, and was able to determine where the private swearing in ceremony was to be held. He had his bomb, made similar to the two other ones, was able to hear, and knew where to land the bomb in a matter of minutes. The effect would be devastating, and the entire nation would be in shock. It would not be forgotten ever.

The time or place of the swearing in had not been announced. Nell heard it from his instruments and confirmed that it was correct. It would be in a remote building at 2:30 and would be witnessed by only a few official people, who had not been identified. That was perfect. He would launch the bomb and have it land at about 2:35. If it worked, the United States would never be the same.

At 2:31 in the afternoon, Nell released his bomb. At 2:33, it was tracked and followed by the United States Air Force. They let it go. They could easily have destroyed it. And at 2:34, it crashed into the remote building at Moon River, destroying it. Nell thought he did it. No notice was given on the news because they did not know the time or place.

The entire force of the United States went into action. They knew from where the bomb had been sent before it even landed. They made noises as if it had hit its exact target, and the panic was real. Nothing yet was televised to the nation, but the attack on the killer squad was in progress. When the apartment was breached, it was a total surprise, and Nell had no time to reach for his poison. An army of the best-fighting men in the world swarmed over his little den, and he was so surprised that he simply surrendered without even trying to destroy his arsenal. They had him with all his paraphernalia intact, and they started logging it while he was still there. Three bombs, and one total victory.

They blindfolded him and gave no hint who he was. Within minutes, he was taken to a secure location, while the best men in the business were going full tilt over his location. They were especially looking for a connection to someone, anyone, and being careful enough to try not to trigger a connection in case it was possible that Nell's capture itself gave the whole thing away. Being careful was an understatement.

Looking out for a terrorist plot was one primary connection, except that the entire world had gone silent for days before the attack. That was curious. There was no obvious connection to anyone in the world, and the equipment was good but could have been put together by half-a-dozen-skilled people. Analysis of the equipment continued and would continue until some connection emerged.

Bassoon heard the news from the second bedroom, and Bassoon raced to it. Only certain agents were admitted. It looked amazing with all the important landmarks clearly visible. It was impossible that they would not be able to learn something from this operation.

Top-level people convened and decided on action. With no one knowing, they quickly swore in the speaker of the House, and at last, they had a president. They then announced her, with great fanfare, and announced that she would address the nation in a half hour. They kept the capture of Nell a secret for as long as possible, but they knew it wouldn't last long, and they hoped it would last at least till the speaker of the House spoke.

When the speaker of the House spoke, she did not say, "My fellow Americans." She said, "My dear Americans," and declared a week of mourning. She was touching, spoke warmly of the president and vice president, and was comforting to lots of people. The efforts that went on during her brief talk were chilling.

By the next morning, the news had broken about Nell's capture, the fake swearing in, and the phony explosion, and the news was about nothing else. People were glued to their sets. CNN, CNBC, and Fox were all over it, and newsmen and newswomen were trying to get any senior official they could find.

Bassoon was trying to learn what he could from the second bedroom. To say it was complex was an understatement. It was state of the art, with all kinds of bells and whistles, and it was all done in English and good English at that. And there was no way to tell who gave the commands or edicts. There was no way to reconnect to the mastermind and no apparent way to contact him. The entire process seemed to exist by itself in the ether, and there was no way connect it to anyone.

The people questioning Nell were extremely careful. They tried every way they knew how to ask who gave the orders, and Nell simply said nothing. They told him everything, but nothing seemed to work. His hands and feet were secure, and they were afraid he would try to kill himself if given half the chance.

Bassoon concentrated on the makeup of the second bedroom. To say it was impressive was an understatement. He studied it from every angle, from top to bottom, and impressive as it was, it was impossible to put it together without a connection. He became more and more worried about it as he went. He called and talked to Waters, and Waters knew what he was going to say before he said it. When Waters was sure that Bassoon could do no more, he told him that he should go back to FBI headquarters.

Publicity from the new day's events was mind-boggling. Every paper and publication reviewed the tragic events, and there were plenty of theories about who had given the orders. Remarkably, no one claimed responsibility, and that fact gave support to more bizarre theories.

The thinking was that there might be another blow, and nothing was planned that was not canceled or called off. Life slowed to a halt, and everyone was focused on the TV. People were plain scared. All sorts of crank calls were received at every location, and everyone had to be eliminated. Slowly, people began to adapt, and things sort of went back to normal.

Waters called Bassoon and sat down with him and had a long chat. He talked slowly, always thinking, and paced back-and-forth before the window.

"Andy," he said, "there has to be an explanation, and we have to think outside the box. Suppose the bombs had been made and attached to the podia before the day even came, maybe long before. Suppose they were detonated by something in the podium or even by the spoken word, 'My fellow Americans' was a good place to start, and what tragic irony if that were the trigger. The people who did this could have done it long beforehand, and that's why we weren't able to catch them or even see them in the act. We are looking through the footage and finding nothing."

Andy was thinking along the same lines. "Where would I start?" he said. "I could try to see if something was put in place beforehand, but how could I know where to start?"

"Well, you could get a hold of that podium, track everything that was done to it for some period, and see if you could find the fixing of the bomb. It had to be done somewhere," he said.

"I could look at the entire history of the podium, but that got to be too long," said Bassoon. "Let's pick a hypothetical date, say three months, and see if we get anything. If we do, we're golden. All we need is a break."

"And if you do," said Waters, "and it enables you to focus on a person or persons, then we start to have something."

"Well, I could start with that, and then adjust it if need be. Do you know where the podium was and how it was chosen? Is it possible it was taken at random? If it was, then the bomb might have been placed very close to the actual date, and things might prove easier," said Bassoon.

"Right now, I don't know that," said Waters. "It's a good pace to start. Let me know whatever you need, and you'll have it. Keep me posted."

THE CHASE

Andy called the FBI agents at the United Nations, told them what he was doing, and hopped on a plane back to New York. He would finally be able to sleep in his own bed tonight, and he ached to see his wife. It was only a few days, but it seemed like a lifetime. When they finally met, he hugged her for a long time, and he wanted to undress her right then, but he waited until the night was silent, and in the meantime, he reunited with his children. To say they were happy to see him was an understatement.

He was given a room, all the records about the podia, and hours of videotapes, and two FBI agents told him they would help if needed. He didn't make them ask twice, and the three began plowing through hours of materials. It was pure drudgery. He was looking for the precise podium, which meant working backward, starting with the first one that blew up. First, he had to have a way to identify the correct podium, and that was no easy task. It appeared at first glance that the podium was simply been pulled out of storage and checked for additions to it, but a close look gave him something. The one that blew up had a slight mark visible on the right side—almost certainly just a mark from use—and he blew up the mark many times so he could identify it. Then he had to find the mark on the other podia.

Finally, he thought he found the mark on one of the tapes. Blown up, it looked identical. It appeared on a picture that was about six weeks old. Painstakingly, he had to search all the photos of use, to find the right one, and he slowly did, putting all the photos in order.

The problem was that he had no way to know if he missed a picture or pictures of the right podium, and only one would be the right one.

The other FBI agents were looking through all the other photos, and they kept a pile of the ones that had the right side obliterated or covered, such that it might be the right one. They then winnowed down all pictures that might be the right one. It took hours and hours. At last, one of the other agents screamed something, and Bassoon knew he found it. It was a day and a half before the explosion, and the camera just caught a guy, very blurry, pull the podium out, appear to arrange something on its underside, and place the podium in a place where it would be likely to be chosen. Each picture of the slide was blown up and analyzed. The exact podium was selected by the secret service for use the morning of the explosion, and it was checked by the secret service's electronic gear, but nothing was found.

The picture of the man was checked on every single web page known to man, and nothing was found, except for one picture of a man going through a turnstile too fast two years earlier. Bingo. They had him.

Bassoon hopped on a plane back to Washington to give the news to Waters in person. The man's name was Marion, and there was precious little on him. He was American, born and raised in the Midwest, middle-aged, and there was almost nothing in his file. That was odd. He had a few odd jobs in car repair, lived lots of places, but no attachments of any kind, marital or otherwise. There was nothing about his family, no sources to ask about. He did file taxes, but nothing unusual, and he apparently signed the returns himself. He was a good American, but private and almost conscious of it. And nothing on any website.

Waters listened and considered. A loner. No record. The one thing that was sure was that he had been the one who placed the bomb, so he was as dangerous as could be. Curiously, there was nothing giving away any connection to any kind of terrorist organization, even indirectly, so there was no way to know who he was working for. Agents were all over contacts between him and any bank in the world, and so far no luck. And no connections to any organization that could arm him or get him what he needed to make the delicate bomb. It was as if he had made it up himself.

"Bassoon," Waters said, "there have to be some connections, so let's assume that he has a connection to some big group. His paucity of a record must be on purpose."

"That's a big assumption," Bassoon said, "but one that won't necessarily cut us off. If anything, it'll keep everything open."

"Right," said Waters, "so let's work with it. Andy, you've got to find him and watch him, to see who he connects to. We're not looking for other lowlifes. We're looking for bosses. When you find him, which shouldn't be too hard, you have to keep him under surveillance until you see him contact someone from whom he takes orders. Then we can decide what to do with him. If we have to take him, we will."

It all sounded good to Bassoon, so he needed to find him. That part was inevitable, but no way to know how to do it.

"So, Evans, how do you think I should find him?"

Waters thought. He said, "Well, it can be any form of transportation, or none at all. You have to figure out what he did after the bomb exploded. First, check every form of payment for anything whatsoever and every kind of picture on every line. I'll get a team to help you. When you find him, stay close, keep an army of backup, and see if he makes any move like he wants some orders. By the way, if he has gone international, that's somewhat different, and we'll have to figure it out when we see it."

Bassoon was in thought. "Evans, what are you going to do to try to find out the sequence of the vice president's bomb? It must have been different."

"I thought of that," said Waters. I'll go through the same sort of process with other agents, and they will try to find out how the Washington bomb was made, by whom, and how the two bombs are connected. We'll keep the two processes interactive, and they will interact with you. But right now, you are ahead of the curve. Don't lose sight of that."

"Okay," said Bassoon.

Bassoon was cautious. At last, he had something he could work with. But he was able to find no pictures of any kind with Alright if that was his name. Bassoon thought for a long second what would happen if he was not among any pictures—suppose he was dead—but there was no point in considering that unless there were nothing. The fact that so many pictures were everywhere nowadays made it virtually impossible that his fact would not show up somewhere. He just had to find it.

So he kept looking everywhere, and it was pure drudgery. He looked every possible place in the days after the bomb, at street corners and highways, and there was nothing. It was getting so tedious that he had to stop. He looked at rental cars, bus stations, train stations, and photos from rest stops on highways. He examined all the photos from marinas and all the photos from airports. He started to think that the individual had hidden himself in a cave. But then there was something. In a grainy photo from a highway rest stop was a blurry picture that just might be the one. The man was headed for the restroom. Maybe he found it.

He collected all the photos from that restroom, looked at them all, but found no more. Just one grainy photo; well, that would be enough. He went out to that highway rest stop, looked at every photo, and quietly asked questions of every man who was there. No one knew anything, but they tried to be helpful, and at least he knew that Alright was going west. He was being very careful. But after all, to go westward from central Pennsylvania left almost the entire nation in his course.

He retraced the steps to the highway rest stop and found nothing. More importantly, he found nothing at all at any locations after that stop. He figured that there had to be more rest stops, if there were any after the first one, so he assumed that Alright stopped at some place within a car's ride of the first one. That made a giant circle around the rest stop, a circle that included the cities of Pittsburgh,

Cincinnati, and Columbus, unless of course he planned to stay a night or two at some place within that group and then move on. Alright made no more pictures he could find at any time after the first one.

Mr. Alright was not shocked after hearing the news about Nell. He always thought it was idiotic to try for, but he let the bigwigs try to pull off the unimaginable. Nell's name was never used in the story, so Alright didn't know if they knew it. He was just glad he had been careful and hoped to hell Orvitz and Wassit had been too, and he knew above all else, it was critical to be cautious. So he waited. He didn't dare contact his superiors—they'd probably just kill him—and he sure as hell didn't want to contact Orvitz or Wassit. He knew that it was important not to allow any pictures to be taken of him, and he started to go batty just sitting in his cave. He knew that he had to go out.

So he thought about how to do it. All the stores had cameras, and there was nothing he wanted more than walking calmly into a local store. He put on a blond wig, mustache, and appropriated a slight limp. He wore a hat over the wig. He practiced moving. When he felt comfortable, he ventured outside, and he felt great. He slowly walked to the local bodega and tried to remember to keep his face covered when he knew he was before a camera. He realized he could never know all the time. He shopped at the store, bought some beer and things he needed, kept his face hidden at the cash register, and paid cash. It was fairly easy. He was ecstatic, and he felt liberated back in his den. He thought about going out to a bar, thought better of it, and was content to save it for another day.

He ventured out like that from time to time, always being careful. He had a hidden gun, just in case, but he knew that he was probably dead the moment he had to use it. At last, he got a call. His apartment came with a host of burner phones, and he had practiced using one per call. "Hello," he said.

"Congrats," said the other caller, "two out of three isn't bad."

"Yeah, well, two out of three ain't perfection, and who knows what they were able to learn from Nell. What do you hear?" he asked.

"Not much," came the answer, and it prompted a host of other questions that he kept to himself. "Stay calm and cool, and we'll call you again."

And the caller hung up. Alright smiled. All the local color gave him some amusement, and he turned back on the television. He put the burner phone where he would never use it again.

THE CAPTURE

He became slightly more comfortable as he waited. He went out a few times, always very carefully, with his disguise on and his gun hidden. He did not go out late at night because that would be too dangerous, and he always went close to his apartment. It did not take long for him to be spotted, especially by the ones who were giving him orders. They watched him. When he went behind a corner, where there was no one around for a few seconds, a quick man with a hoodie smiled at him and pumped two silent bullets into his head. Just like that, he was dead. The killer took only a few seconds to take everything out of his pockets, including his apartment key and his meager identification, and left him dead as if he was robbed. It was simple and easy.

Alright's death was not known for some time. He was put in the morgue, and because there was no one to claim him, was scheduled to be buried in potter's field. The only key was that it had been listed a homicide although no one was found, and a low-level FBI person had been looking through all the suspicious deaths and miraculously found him. He was recognizable, and Bassoon went out to see him to concretely identify him. He was taken back to DC and held for some time until everyone was sure he wasn't needed. No one ever found his apartment, and it was a nagging blank for some time. No one who killed him was ever found.

Alright's death aggravated Bassoon, but he knew it was a lost cause. His superiors had known where to find him, and they knew he was a liability. There was no point looking for his killer, so Bassoon moved on to the next step. Which was what exactly?

Bassoon felt like he had come up empty and wasn't sure where to go. The obvious point was to try to break into the efforts being made by the Washington team, which is what he decided to do. First, he had to brief Waters and get his okay.

He talked to Waters at length. "I struck out," said Bassoon, "and I'm not happy about it."

"Well," replied Waters, "you didn't really strike out. They just found Alright ahead of you, and they told us that, whoever they are, they are an organized bunch. You have to stay on it. I'll get you involved in the Washington effort. You know Rodgers, don't you? He's in charge of Washington, and it's quite a mess."

"How so?" asked Bassoon.

"They started looking for a podium, thought they found one, talked to the secret service man who they saw on the video, and found out it was just a standard check of the group of podia. I checked out the secret service man, and he was okay. No harm, no foul. So they started looking again, and they have found nothing. Very frustrating," said Waters.

"All right," Bassoon said, "I'll help them. They have to find something."

"I'll get you plugged into the Washington group," said Waters.

Bassoon walked into the Washington group, introduced himself, and immediately learned what frustration felt like.

"Hi, Bassoon," said Aaron Rodgers, "we can sure use some help."

"Glad to help," said Bassoon. "Show me what you've got."

Washington was a mess. There was a false lead when they thought they found someone, but it was a false alarm. So Bassoon decided to look at the pictures again. Rodgers said okay and dumped on him the tremendous amount of already-used photos. Bassoon was dumbfounded and didn't know what to do, so he started going through the pictures again. It involved Washington pictures, so there were lots of kinds unlike in New York. He saw all kinds of normal-looking ones, just showing podia taken and kept in storage. There was a more or less standard way to do it, so the many standard ones just looked normal. He thought it was getting hopeless.

But one normal-looking one did get his attention. It was during a standard-looking check of the podia and took place when others were in the storage room. There seemed to be no effort to hide the process, which is why it looked normal. There was also no effort to hide the face of the official woman. She was wearing official clothing and looked completely normal, and she did not show any sign of doing anything improper. But closer examination did show something funny. Without showing any sign of doing anything and without changing speeds, she did turn the podium upside down and put something in its place. She sure looked calm. She stayed that way while she turned the podia upside down one more time, finished it, put it down, and moved on at the same speed to fix another one. Again, she repeated the same routine, calmly put down the podium, and moved on.

Bassoon looked several times at the ritual. He zoomed in closely so he could get a look at the substance being affixed to the podium but couldn't quite get a fix on it. He asked a programmer to help him, but no clear picture of the substance followed. He was told it could just as well be a cleaning fluid, or it could be something else, but there was no way to tell.

He showed the pictures to Waters and explained his thinking. "What if she put something under it?" he said.

"You mean like a bomb? It doesn't look anything like that. And she doesn't look nervous or mind if anyone is watching at all," Waters said.

"Well, maybe she's just really good," Bassoon said. "And remember, we don't know what the hell the bomb is supposed to look like going in."

Waters thought for a long time. Then he said, "What do you know about her?"

"I looked her up on the computer, and there isn't much. Bannita Wassit is her name, and she's been there about three months. She lives in the district, not married, and really loves the job. Perfectly normal," he said.

"That's odd," said Waters, "seems too perfect. Let's see if we can find out anything more."

So they called the secret service chief, told him why, and put the question. He called them back and told them to come right down. He had a fairly senior member with him. The three of them looked carefully at the pictures and, at first, saw nothing unusual. But with a closer look, the senior member saw something small sticking out from behind the substance. She simply showed no sign of giving away the truth. They blew up the one picture with the anomaly, and there it was. Tucked in behind the podia was a bomb, hidden as well as anything could be, and it miraculously only took seconds to fix it. If she hadn't been so good at hiding it, it would have shown sooner.

There was incredulity at the depth of the bomb, with apparent sensitivity to the words *my fellow Americans*. That was apparently set in the bomb, to go off, and it would last as long as the bomb sat and waited, even if it took a long time. Ingenious. Set by a truly expert bomb maker.

So they had the bomb and the bomb maker or at least the bomb affixer. They looked up her address; they had it because she was employed by the good guys, and they quickly raided her apartment. Nothing. It showed an unremarkably normal home, lived in by an unremarkable woman, with an unremarkable past. She had an unremarkable series of identities, all of which turned out to be false. She had simply disappeared the day of the bombing and vanished without a trace. But where had she gone.

Bassoon knew that the question duplicated the one from the other bombing, but the pursuit of it had to be different. The FBI had to keep the knowledge a secret if it had not already gotten out. Every person who knew about the bombing was checked again, and thankfully, there was no leakage. It was kept very secretive. Bassoon was told to keep it that way.

He was given two top FBI agents who were told to keep it all secret and to recheck the pictures they had of Marion. Nothing. There were simply no pictures of the girl, Bannita Wassit. So he checked from the beginning for any pictures of Wassit and found nothing. This time, he checked pictures starting at her home, and he saw some going to work but nothing unusual and nothing from the day of the bombing. Then he checked the day of the bombing and found nothing, and suddenly he had an idea. The last day she was at work was the day before the bombing, and she suddenly disappeared. So he checked all the photos from the District of Columbia, and voila, he found one. It clearly showed her at Union Station, boarding a train for New York. Bingo.

He had her. So he looked for pictures of her getting off the train in New York, and he found one grainy picture of her, looking somewhat different. She had her hair fixed way up, with glasses, and a collar turn way up so when she looked down, she was hidden. He saw a second picture of her leaving the station, and then he lost her in the din of the city. She was apparently there the day of the double bombing.

He had to talk with Waters. He went back to the FBI headquarters and laid it all out.

"She was in New York the day of the bombings apparently keeping low, and we can guess that she left with Alright," said Waters. "But we can't find any pictures of them leaving together," he said. "They must have had a car," he said after thinking. "But she was not with him the day he stopped at the gas station. So he must have dropped her off someplace before that."

"This is getting tricky," said Bassoon, "and there is too much we don't really know and are surmising. What if we are wrong?

"Well, if we are wrong about something, we just have to back up and fix it," answered Waters. "We have to go with what we have. I'll grant you that it leaves a big hole in what we know before Alright is alone at the gas station. What we should do is draw a big circle around the area from the train station to the place where the gas station is and surmise that she stopped in there or that she is still inside that circle. If she's inside that circle, we'll never find her, but if she left, we might get a picture in a bus stop, train station, airplane hangar, boat marina, or other car. So we know what to look for. That's what you've got," he said. "What do you think?"

"I think is sounds good," said Bassoon. "But if it comes up empty, we have to remember to go back to the beginning."

So Waters arranged to get all the thousands of pictures to be reviewed, Bassoon went back to New York, got enough FBI agents to help him review them, and got down to work.

To say it was tedious is a big understatement. Looking through pictures of all the bus stops seemed hopeless. But Bassoon said he wanted it done day by day, starting with the day before the explosions. They felt somewhat hopeless, as they went to the second day, but there was something interesting early in the morning of the second day, in a picture of the Greyhound bus station in, of all places, Poughkeepsie, New York. It was only a partial shot of a woman, trying to keep from being seen, but after all, no one could keep from the shots of every single camera trying to take pictures of every single person, leaving every single bus station in the country. Her head was turned, her hair was up, she had on a baseball cap and glasses, but she looked partly familiar with the picture of her at the train station in New York.

They carefully compared the two pictures and concluded that they might be of the same person. If so, she was on her way to Pittsburgh, again with no stops. He looked, saw the same kind of partial picture getting off the bus in downtown Pittsburgh, and figured he probably had her, at least as much as getting where she was going on the day of the bombings. He headed toward Pittsburgh. That is, he headed there with two expert FBI agents, who were supposed to keep him safe.

The agents were Abe Robertson and Steve Wilson, both white, in their thirties, with a good deal of strength in their past, and solid agents. Bassoon was glad to have them. When they arrived in Pittsburgh, they told no one, not wanting to set off any bells, and they checked into the hotel. They settled down and began looking through pictures to see if they could find her, and they came up empty. That was expected. She was too good for that, and Bassoon felt in his bones that she was still somewhere in Pittsburgh. Pittsburgh was a small enough place, so it wasn't that hard in theory to search for her, and they split up the city to try to find her.

Bassoon got the central city, so he walked around, looking like a tourist, going nowhere in particular, to get his bearings. He got comfortable. He started hanging out in coffee shops and computer shops. He kept his eyes open and his cell phone always on. He frequently checked with his two compadres, who were doing the same thing. A girl who looked happy-go-lucky saw him from a distance, knew who he was, smiled slightly, and moved toward him. He didn't see her. When she was ten feet away, she took out a gun with a silencer and carelessly prepared to fire it. Just then, a waitress slipped, dropped her tray, and was right in front of him as she fell. The two bullets grazed her shoulder, and she fell with a grunt in a split second. As he looked at her and realized she was shot, he wheeled and pulled out his gun, looking in the opposite direction. The shooter was gone. He stooped and helped the waitress, saw the wounds were not life threatening, and called for an ambulance and for Abe and Steve.

It all happened so fast that it almost seemed like a dream. Bassoon quickly recovered, realized he was almost shot, and started thinking crazy thoughts like that they knew who he was. That was almost impossible. How could they know that? Either they knew the inside scoop of the FBI or one of their own people was a traitor. Either one was bad. He called Waters right there and was none too happy, and Waters said to go back to the room and call him from there. When he did, he was somewhat more relaxed and was thinking rationally.

"How the hell could they know who I was," said Bassoon, "when I was just one of lots of FBI agents looking for them?"

"Well, they probably knew who you are from knowing a whole list of agents who would be chasing them," said Walters, who thought that their knowledge was somewhat less damaging than did Bassoon. But Walters said that, that fact made him sure that, whoever it was, it was affiliated with a substantial enemy.

Bassoon knew he was right.

On another continent, it was late at night, and all the lights of Saint Petersburg looked beautiful. His Honor Mr. Ivanov looked serene and happy. He had no bodyguards with him because he told them to wait at the hotel, but his appearance alone gave him what he wanted. He sat in a bar, with nothing at all on the table, way in the corner where he could not be seen. His old KGB friend, Nikolas

Rohab, walked in, and he caused him to be searched from his top to his bottom, before giving him a hug. They ordered the best vodka the place had, and they drank it profusely. They laughed about old times, until Ivanov got serious. They knew that only three people knew what they were talking about, and they both knew that their lives depended on that.

"It's amazing," said Rohab, "what a dramatic effect it had. Sometimes I can't believe it."

"We've done it," said Ivanov, "and the world will never be the same."

"What about Nell?" asked Rohab.

"Well, I don't think he talked at all, and his family is with us and safe, being watched twenty-four hours a day. He is the best agent we have, and it is inconceivable that he would talk," said Ivanov.

"You really should grant yourself a great victory," said Rohab.

"I plan to," Ivanov said, and they both laughed.

"Are you going over to express condolences?" Rohab asked.

"I'll wait to see what it looks like, but not too soon," Ivanov answered.

It was a monumental victory, and neither one wanted to break the spell.

Then they got serious. They knew there was much to discuss, and neither one was in any hurry.

"How do you feel about Wassit and Orvitz?" Rohab asked.

"Well, we are trusting them, for now," said Ivanov. "We will watch and listen, and if more is required, we are ready. The beauty is that none of our other agents know of the whole plot, so none are truly dangerous. When the time is right, we will be able to get them out."

Bassoon quickly recovered and spent his time looking at the video himself in the café. It wasn't very good because neither one was really in range, but it did show that the shooter was a woman. He just couldn't be sure that it was the same woman he had seen on the videos from the bus stations, but he gave credibility to the assumption that, that was right. If so, the woman was now looking for him, and that baffled him. Why? It made no sense, unless of course she just happened to see him and thought it would be prudent to take the chance. That is the hypothesis he was going with.

"You have to be careful," said Abe, "because she is ruthless."

"Well," said Bassoon, "there's nothing about this situation that's not, so we have to remember we're in the gravest danger, so we shouldn't be doing anything alone."

"Copy that," said Abe.

Wassit was upset. She had acted on instinct, been unsuccessful, and perhaps given the thing away. Well, she thought, instinct usually saved her, and she was convinced to use it to the full extent. She left her apartment, wore her disguise, and got the quickest train she could get due north. If she was lucky, they wouldn't know she was on it, and if she was not, it wouldn't matter.

She got off at Lake Erie, Pennsylvania, and slowly worked her way down to the docks. She picked out a suitable vessel and waited till it was late at night. She slowly moved away from the harbor, keeping her head hidden, and when she was out of range, she started up the engine. She smiled slightly. She knew that it could fail in an instant, if she saw an engine from the coast guard, but until then, she was determined. She also knew that the boat would be reported as stolen, perhaps as early as the next morning, and she would have to be off the boat and be gone quickly.

She crossed until she saw the shore early in the morning and landed a half mile from the nearest town. Now she was looking for the Mounted Police. She took the boat down and put the big mast flat and covered it as best she could and quickly left the lake. Then, when she got into town, she took off her disguise and appeared different and liberated. The only issue now was whether she could get on a plane out of the country in time.

Hassad Orvitz was keeping a low profile. Little did anyone know that he was a double agent. Indeed, it had been years since he had contacted anyone on the Arabic team, and he was not going to do so now. But he had to savor the relationships, and Bannita's anxiety was especially joyful. He had a friend let him know that she had gotten on a train to Lake Eerie, and he knew she would be trying to leave the country. He thought about what he should do. On one hand, if she got back to Russia, he would stay safe and be hidden. On the other hand, if he had her killed, the degree of safety would be assured, he would remain hidden, and the rest of the plot would unfold safely. His decision was easy.

He bought for a cash telephone at a local Rochester store and made a single phone call to an eerie number. He spoke in code, and in it, he ordered the hit. It was to be clean, quick, and not connected to anyone or thing. It was to be like a robbery and was to leave no clue behind. The person he called said okay. He discarded the phone and went back to living the disguised life.

Wassit was found dead, an apparent robbery victim, a day and a half later. She was found in an alley behind a dumpster, with no papers or identification, and kept in an unknown status for several days. The FBI then found her, knew who she was, and brought her back to Washington, a few days after that.

It rattled both Bassoon and Waters and meant what they had known all along: the entire plan was engineered from the very top of a very sophisticated entity, and their plan had been well thought out from the start. The only chance was now through Nell, and they both knew that he was little help.

As for the trial, Larry Robinson was the best prosecutor they had. He was a lifer, forty-two, from Harvard Law School, and had risen inside the justice department for twelve years. He came from the big firm Driscoll & Birman and never looked back, wanting to be a federal prosecutor his whole life. He was married, with no children, lived in Bethesda, and spent all his time at the department. He was already looking at Nell. He talked about him to the attorney general, who had processed it with the new President, and understood that, if there was to be a prosecution, he was to be the man. He was eager to get started.

There were enormous things to consider. First, the case was to be the most important one ever brought. He could pick his team—which had to be substantial—and it had to stay on it forever. Second, it was presumed that, whoever it would turn out to have given the orders, it was the largest and most organized group in the world. And third, Nell would probably do no talking. All that, and the prosecution had to be successful.

Robinson studied the pictures from the second bedroom and spent time studying the actual bedroom, which had been maintained and guarded zealously since the attack on the speaker of the House. It was quite a setup. It was so detailed that it must have been designed by someone with top-level intelligence or by someone with extensive knowledge of the seventy-five-mile area. Robinson's bet was on the latter person. In fact, no one could have designed the whole area by himself or herself. He had to have had a detailed map or a picture of the entire area.

With that background, it was impossible to guess anyone other than a foreign country. Any country, including all the Arab countries with hostility. In fact, they were the first candidates. Robinson thought that Iran or its progeny was a good place to start, and he was given full access to all accusatory stuff they already had on Iran. He went through all of it.

Meantime, he thought about who his team would be. His second chair would be Stuart Oleman, a lifer who was forty-six years old; Shelley Pistelson, Robinson's favorite assistant; and Robinson, who picked up the phone and called Fred Walright, then a partner at Driscoll & Birman, who said yes before the question was even asked. Those four lawyers would be team who would go down in history as breaking, or losing, the biggest case ever brought.

They took an office which was an entire floor of the justice department, next to the attorney general. There was a small back office setup with four beds, in case any of them would ever need to sleep there. And all the stuff from the bedroom was copied to a tee and put right in the middle of their floor. Their floor was made bulletproof and guarded twenty-four hours a day by the marines.

Robinson knew he would need a crackerjack group of investigators, so he talked about it with Waters and heard right away about Bassoon. He looked up Bassoon and liked what he saw. He talked to Bassoon and liked him after thirty seconds and welcomed him aboard. He said one investigator would probably not be enough, so

Bassoon recommended Abe Robinson and Steve Wilson, and they had the beginning of a squad. They only needed to know what to do.

So they prepared to try Nell. But they had no proof. They did have the failed bomb attempt—it even killed some people—but what they wanted was liability for the double murders of the president and vice president and primarily, who was responsible. And this, they had no proof of whatever.

Nell simply would not talk. They offered to take life off the table. They tried to offer sanctuary to his immediate family—whoever that was—but he wouldn't talk about them or even make the offer seem palatable. They couldn't even tell for sure what nationality he belonged to or what his lineage was. They were stumped. So they repeatedly postponed his trial.

And worse than that, they did not even know about the third man in the cabal or what role he had connecting the two assassinations.

Bassoon was involved in all these discussions, and he did not have a clue. In fact, he was the one who kept repeating that the trial should be put off. He knew that there was a big piece of the puzzle they were missing.

What to do? He sat and tried to talk it through with Waters.

"Evans, we don't even have a cogent theory about what happened," he said. "And the detail on the maps we found in Nell's apartment is so great that, that level of knowledge could only have come from the country that gave the orders. We are missing it."

"I know it," said Waters. "But keep looking at the little facts instead of the big picture. Is there a person or persons we are missing? Were the two horrific assassinations coordinated? They must have been. What's the connection? What are we missing?"

"Remember, we don't know how the two assassins, they were both killed, met or how they left New York. We don't even know who was with them or who was giving the orders. We only know the objective facts," said Bassoon. "How do we learn what really happened?"

"I just don't know," said Waters. "I just don't know. If you could find a third person or persons or a way that the orders were transmitted, we just might have something."

In a word, they were stumped.

Waters scratched his chin. "Is there some way you could find out if there was a third person or persons?" he said.

"I don't know," said Bassoon.

"You know," said Waters, "we only have Wassit alone going onto the train in Poughkeepsie. How did she get there? Did someone drop her off? Where did they go?"

"I'm sure I checked all the videotape that brought her there," said Bassoon. "I'll check it again."

So Bassoon revisited the videotape. But what was it? There was nothing to revisit. There was no videotape of Wassit getting to the Poughkeepsie train station at all. That seemed a tad odd. She was either dropped off, or disembarked from a cab or bus, or got there some other way. Why was there no picture? Could it be that someone tried to keep it secret?

Bassoon had an idea. He wanted to check rent-a-cars. It was a long shot, so he zeroed in on the rentals in the week or so before the assassinations.

He looked everywhere. He looked in New York. He looked in Washington. He found nothing. He looked at cars rented by a single man. Cars rented by a single woman. He looked at so many that he couldn't look any more. He gave up. But then he thought about cars that were rented in one place and returned in another. There were less of those, but still a lot. How would he know? He looked at cars rented anywhere in the east and could then have driven to the spot on Route 80 where he knew the car stopped. There were less of those. And by the way, where were they going? He knew they found one of the men—actually she was a woman—in Pittsburgh. So he looked in Pittsburgh. Nothing. It remained to check every spot east or north of there. That was impossible. He was stumped.

Marion had been found in Cincinnati. So he looked there, and eureka! He spelled his name differently, but there it was. He returned it about a week after the first killing, he impounded it, and it had miles that could have driven to there. It came from New York, and then he found from where it was taken. It was rented by a man named Alright, who paid cash for it. No wonder it hadn't raised an eyebrow.

So Alright had driven the whole way to Cincinnati, but he had no idea how many people he had dropped off. Pittsburgh was clearly on the way, so he might have dropped off Wassit, but God knew how many others he might have taken.

He looked again at the Poughkeepsie film. There was no way to tell if anyone else had gotten out of the car. Indeed, there was no way to know if any other human being had gotten out of that car.

Bassoon was stumped. But wait a minute. Wassit turned up in Pittsburgh. She must have traveled there in the car with Alright. What if she got out at the train or bus station? He looked again at the video of the train station. Nothing. He looked at the video of the Poughkeepsie bus station. It was grainy and obtuse, but there she was. She wasn't apparent until she was just inside of the bus station, but there she was. That meant that she got out of the car driven by Alright. Oh, if Alright only dropped off someone else, they would have him.

He looked again at the video of the Poughkeepsie train station. At about the same time as Wassit got out at the bus station, there were three single men getting out at the train station. He looked more closely. Two of the men had gotten out of cars that appeared in the video at the front of the station. The cars did not match the one that Alright drove to Cincinnati. But the third one did not come from a car that was anywhere within the video. His head was shot from the side, but it was a fairly good shot. It meant that maybe he found the third man. But how would he know?

He went to see Waters. He summarized all the foregoing. Waters was silent for a moment and then spoke,

"Bassoon, you are brilliant. You have done it and broken the missing link. Let's find out who he is, what he is, what country he represents, and what compatriots he may have. Focus everything on him."

"Okay," said Bassoon, "let's go."

They made the picture of him the key and copied it a million times and distributed it to everyone, including the media. They got all kinds of supposed leads, and they chased down everyone. They searched copies of every conceivable database. They searched every copy of every possible citizenship member they had. They found nothing.

He was an unknown person. They asked every member of the underground spies, but no one knew him. Waters said that, that was to be expected—if he was as central as they thought—since his country wanted to make it as hard as possible to figure out who he was.

Ivanov was carefully watching. He was very afraid to try anything more, for fear of giving himself away. But he was getting nervous. He didn't know what he would do if they were going to start to try Nell, and every minute was a precarious risk. He talked to Nicholas Rohab.

"I think I should make a move," he said, "because it's less risky than sitting and watching. Things could only get worse."

"Okay," said Rohab, "it's probably time to move."

So Ivanov clandestinely reached out to his special agent, Orvitz. Orvitz was calmly waiting for instructions and of course, never did anything that would ever give away his double-agent status. He was ready to hear instructions, and he calmly listened to them.

Nell was getting too dangerous to risk. Ivanov thought it was time to take him out. It had no time sensitivity; it had to be done right, and above all, if Orvitz was caught, he had to take himself out and not reveal where the orders came from. Orvitz understood, was calm, silently was happy, and quietly was glad he had no prior experience. His secret double agency was a huge secret.

THE SET-UP

So Orvitz had his instructions and was free to think about it. He was not to interfere with another agent.

The Americans thought they knew Orvitz but did not know what his name was. They would not hesitate to grab him if they could.

At the same time, it was something to worry about. He thought about the cycle of life that he was involved in. It was extra-extraordinary. He had been born to a Russian father and Turkish mother and raised in a weird mix of orthodoxy and respect. His father was a Russian diplomat, of a mid-level kind, and mother a white-skinned Turk, who was reared in a pro-Russian environment that was modestly anti-Muslim. His appearance was Russian. But his loyalty was pro-Islam, as his closest friends as a child had experienced all the anti-Islam fanaticism that was common in the upper society of that part of the world. He came up inside the pro-Russian community, including the diplomatic corps, and his fealty to the Islamic people was entirely secretive.

He was not married and had no ties to bind him. He was approximately thirty-two, trained in the Russian way, and the word lethal barely described him.

What he had done for the conspiracy was simply unknown. He had organized everything, put the two conspirators together, organized what they did, and kept it a secret. He picked them. And he evacuated with them. In the light of the conspiracy, what he did was absolutely astounding.

Orvitz knew he had to be careful. Every time he went out—which was not too often—he wore a disguise. Little did he know that was the whole ball game.

He wanted to check on how Nell was being kept. It wasn't easy to find. He was in maximum security, kept on suicide watch, and was under personal supervision twenty-four hours a day. His guards were changed every two hours, and two at a time watched him. It was completely under electronic supervision, and every little thing was watched. Getting to him was next to impossible.

What to do? It would, after all, be the height of irony if he was killed after all that he had committed. But it turned out that Nell was taken up and questioned—with all kinds of efforts—a few times a week and in front of his lawyer and others. It was all done by the book, and his federal captors more than once would have liked it if he had been caught out of the country. Protecting him was the height of irony. But getting to him was just not possible.

Orvitz thought long and hard on it. It seemed the only chance was poisoning him, and even that was next to impossible. Orvitz thought it would be possible to put an unnoticeable poison into his food, but how in the world could he get into the kitchen? And who could he ask to do it? He couldn't ask anyone. And he certainly would not risk doing it himself.

What kind of poison would he use? He did his research. There were several that would not be noticed, and a few would even be very quick to take effect. But he would have to be there.

He took his time. Assuming there were a few poisons he could choose from, how could he be sure that they would not be used for other people? He would of course have to be sure that they would be used as part of some nondescript food group—say sugar or butter—and how could he know that it would not be used for someone else or even tasted by a federal agent? It was hard to see how the poison could be limited to Nell.

He needed some way to know that the special poison would not only be undetected but would also be used exclusively for Nell. Something no one else would eat. He needed to know Nell's own diet. Did he have anything special? And he needed to know that while disguising who it was who wanted to know.

He finally decided: He would secretly call upon his Iranian brothers. They were all waiting silently—they did not know all that had happened—and they would be overjoyed to hear from him. He called the one he had called previously, to help him kill Wassit, and began a negotiation. It was joyous.

First, he made it clear that his contacts must keep it secret and disclosed to as few people as possible. Second, he explained what he wanted help with. His contact instantly understood and would have been glad to instantly give up his life for the cause. And lastly, he needed help getting access to the secure facility without anyone knowing.

They discussed exactly what he wanted. He explained exactly what he needed, and his compatriot was only too happy to help. The first thing he wanted was exactly what Nell's schedule was. Even that was relatively difficult, but not impossible, and they soon had it. Next, they discussed what the fatal killer should be, and they had two substances that would do the trick. The hardest part was figuring out how they would set the trap exclusively for Nell and not accidentally getting anyone else. They discussed ad nauseum how they would do it. It was difficult. It would take quite a while. They agreed to do it—giving up their lives if necessary and trusting in Allah for all things. Above all, his compatriot agreed that as few people should be told about it as possible.

Nell did not have any dietary needs. They did not know what his nationality was or what his preferences might be. They tried to learn some, but he was too clever. So they fed him a normal mix while not combining any special things. They did not have any schedule, and each meal was different. And everything he was given was tasted by two agents. They were very careful.

So they needed to crack the system. They thought long and hard about it and decided one way to try it. They needed two active agents, and they could not be sure it would work. Each agent was dressed the same and carried a fatal dose of cyanide, in case he was caught. The good news was that the switch didn't have to be tried if it wasn't possible, and it could always be tried again.

The idea went like this. They would duplicate the truck that brought the food supplies in, and they would know what the supplies should be. They would know all the code words, would know where the materials should go, and would go through all the steps of security system. They would be in the kitchen at the exact time, and once the two agents would taste the food, the secret Iranian agent, laughing at some joke, would slip in the poison. It would be tasteless and virtually impossible to identify. It would cause a heart attack almost instantaneously. The two agents would carry out the charade throughout the delivery and be gone without raising an eye. If the chance did not present itself, they would simply complete the delivery and try it again.

The only difficult decision was what to do with the real delivery of the goods. The two Iranian compatriots looked at each other and then decided to speak.

"Mr. Orvitz," they said, "it won't be hard to handle that. We just need to give the real truck an accident without anyone getting hurt and prevent that truck from getting to the delivery. By the time he calls and says he can't get there, the poison will have been delivered."

"In order to do that, you will have to involve other people," said Orvitz, "and that will be dangerous."

"Well," said the two compatriots, "you can't have everything. It will just have to be. The men who have the job of driving the interfering truck will have the cyanide too."

"So be it," said Orvitz. "It will just have to be."

There was a good deal of practice before the event. The compatriots were all devoted. They created the truck; they practiced recreating the delivery; they timed the accident and practiced it eternally; they practiced giving the code words and all the security rigamarole; and they tried to handle joking with the security men and making the connection. They organized the timing. They were ready.

There was a food delivery scheduled right before dinner. The exact contents of the delivery truck were recreated. They knew the exact timing. At the right time, the real truck crashed with a smaller truck, and the impact was bad enough to ruin the real contents, but not to cause serious injury. The other truck—it looked exactly the same—pulled up to the maximum security prison and went through the security protocol without a hitch. The food contents were carried off and delivered. And the two men were brought into the kitchen with the ordered food. As they delivered all the food and as the dinner for Nell was delivered, they laughed at a sick joke, and he administered the poison.

That's when all hell broke loose. One of the kitchen guards saw it. He rang the security alarm, and it seemed like a thousand security guards descended on them. One of them ate his poison and was dead in an instant. The other one—the one who had messed up—was too slow and was grabbed just before he could take the stuff. Just then, one of the security guards from the damaged truck called and reported what happened, and the jig was up.

The entire maximum security prison went into lockdown. The kitchen was cleared, and everything was preserved. One of the invaders who had been captured was whisked away to an FBI institution, and all sorts of people were notified. One of them was Andy Bassoon.

Bassoon was on a plane within minutes of being notified. He talked to Waters and the members of the prosecution team, and his expertise—that is his knowledge of what might have happened—was of greatest importance. When he reached the prisoner, the man had not been questioned yet at all, and the obligation had been reserved for him. First, he discussed what the FBI agent had learned, and he then delved into the interrogation.

'Sir," he said, "you are here because of what happened. We see that you had a personal cyanide capsule and did not have time to take it. We do not know what country you are from or who gave you your directions. So you will tell us who directed you."

"Praise be to Allah," he said.

Bassoon was stunned. He did not expect to hear about Allah. He doubled down.

"Allah did not protect you," he said, "and he left you alone. You should answer my questions if you know what's good for you."

"Praise be to Allah," he said.

"Who gave you the truck?"

"Praise be to Allah."

"Who prepped you with the food?"

"Praise be to Allah."

"Who prepped you to kill Nell?"

"Praise be to Allah."

Bassoon could see that he would gain little else. He tried one other thing.

"What country gave you the orders?" he asked. A blank stare. He took out a picture of Orvitz—whose name he did not know—and asked, "Do you know this man?"

The agent just shook his head. "No."

At this point, Bassoon felt that he did know him. It was the only response that was different.

Bassoon said, "Wait here," and stepped out of the interrogation room to consult with the other FBI agents that were there."

"Do you think he knows?" Bassoon asked.

All the agents said, "Yes."

Bassoon was thinking very fast and talking slowly. He thought about how to get the agent to tell them who the man was. He thought it would be a tough slog, so he prepared for a long haul.

"Let him wait," said Bassoon.

He called Waters.

"What do you think I should do next?" he said.

Waters was thinking. "If he knows who he is, he probably won't say," said Waters. "You'll have to exhaust all avenues. If he leaves you without anything, you'll probably have to give up, unless you can find another way."

Bassoon had his answer and was not much encouraged. He did hope he could find out who was responsible for Allah being in the mix but did not hold out much chance learning who Orvitz was.

He was right. He got little else and no clue who Orvitz was. He finally gave up.

Orvitz was disappointed. He realized he would probably have to do it himself. So he thought about how to do it. He would have to use a precise rifle and get a good shot, and there was really only one way to do it.

So he made his plans. He still needed help from the other Iranians, but this time, success depended entirely on him.

He waited until nightfall. He snuck up behind the brush, broke open a water vent, and climbed in. He had carefully studied the plans. He traveled almost half mile, until he was virtually on top of the top security section where Nell was. He only needed to pick the right one. He had learned where Nell was supposed to be, but certainty was next to impossible. He crawled to where he had a good view and looked down. All the clothing looked the same on each prisoner, and he took a long time to assure that it was as certain as he could be that this was Nell. He readied his gun, set the sights, and dropped two silent bullets into the back of his neck. Nell looked dead, which was as good as it was going to get.

He slowly crept out of there, which took an eternity. When he reached the opening he had entered, he gave the signal, and an unnoticeable car slowly crept into position. He jumped out, and crawled to the car. It slowly moved away. Then it entered the thorough fare, as the light was starting to come up. No signs had been given that the keepers of the prison had known anything happened. He had finally done it.

When they found the body in the morning, there was silence. They found the opening in the water vent, took all of the fingerprints, saw where the car had come, and knew what had happened. They disciplined the prison guards but were unable to show that they had anything to do with it. Bassoon was sure that Orvitz—he still did not know his name—was responsible. A few days later, Nell's demise was carefully announced, and the response was overwhelming.

Bassoon hung around the security prison, hoping to learn something. He didn't. After the failure of the attack on Nell with the poison food, the guards were somewhat jubilant, but their failure with the rifle shots was painful. They simply didn't know anything.

To some, it seemed like it was over but not to Bassoon, not to Waters, and not to the whole FBI. They believed that Orvitz, whose name they still didn't know, was the linchpin, and they still had no clue who he was or how to get at him. They were stumped. Bassoon thought they might get lucky—heaven knows how—so he made sure that each active FBI agent had a picture.

Meanwhile, Ivanov went crazy. He heard about the failed attempt on Nell's life and was beside himself. He deduced Orvitz's double agency and wanted to question Orvitz about it but knew it would be a profound risk to try to have him killed and held out a slim hope that whoever found him would conclude that he was an Arabian agent. Wouldn't that be a wonderful ending.

Anyway, Ivanov was content to stand still, which in a small way, was to Bassoon's benefit. He thought about it day and night, and his wife thought it was funny the way he obsessed about it. Orvitz knew he was wanted by the FBI and hoped they didn't have his name, but he was afraid to show his face in public. He always used a disguise when he went out—which was rarely—and kept as low a profile as possible.

The good guys still had an Arabian agent—from the failed attempt on Nell's life—and assumed that Orvitz was Arabian. But that assumption was not widely held by Bassoon and the others in the know about the whole affair, who held out the possibility—no, the likelihood—that Orvitz was some kind of double agent. The Arabian agent fairly thought that his life was over and spent his time praying and preparing for Allah. He thought about ending his life. He would never give away Orvitz.

Andy Bassoon was at home thinking about all this. After all this time—it seemed like yesterday—he was nowhere closer to a conclusion. He shared his feelings with his wife.

"I feel like I'm in a dream," he said. "I don't seem to be able to get out of it."

"Well," she said, "it has to come to an end. There has to be an ending, whether you like or not."

"I know," said Bassoon, "but without finding that guy, it feels very much alive to me. He has to be somewhere, someone knows him, and we don't seem to be able to find him. And without him, we don't seem to be able to learn who propagated this crime and who we should hold responsible. It's just killing me."

His wife smiled. "You'll get him," she said. "I know you. You'll get him."

He smiled and kissed her.

Meanwhile, life went on, and he periodically checked in on the still-alive people who kept up the search. They were all, no doubt, in their own quandary about it.

He asked them if they knew where Orvitz lived, and they were unable to say a word about it. That seemed odd, even to them, and they thought that must be either because he was hiding someplace, or he was out of the country, or he was dead. And they had no clue which one was right. If he was in hiding, he had to have help, and they had no clue who that was. The FBI had exhausted its search of what they knew about the connections of the Arabians, and they were stumped.

So Bassoon went on with his life. Until one day, he got a phone call out of the blue, and the caller—it was too quick to trace it—never identified himself.

"I saw someone in Baltimore I thought was the guy you're looking for. He was walking alone, with his head down, and he was wearing a disguise. He was heading toward a bodega, near Main and Nineteenth. Underneath, I think it was him." Then he hung up.

Bassoon quickly turned to action. He told Waters about it and headed for Baltimore. He went to Main and Nineteenth, looked everywhere, and clandestinely went into the bodega. He bought a few things and looked around but did not question the man in the bodega until the FBI could check him out. He was clean. So Bassoon returned to the bodega and calmly asked about the man in the picture. The bodega man perused it but said he did not know him, and Bassoon said thanks and left.

Bassoon simply hung around and kept his eyes open. He saw a street vendor, who looked about a hundred years old, bought something from him, and asked if he had ever seen the man. He thought a long time and then said that there was a man who sort of looked like him, but wore a disguise, and hadn't seen him in a while. When asked where he lived, the man pointed to a three-story building and said he thought the man lived in that area. Bassoon said thanks and walked away.

Bassoon found a small apartment that looked well lived in but no one home. He searched it painstakingly but found nothing. He couldn't even be sure Orvitz was living there. But then he found a small clue. It was a printout of a bus schedule to Memphis. The entry for two days earlier was circled.

Bassoon went to Memphis with Waters's blessing. He located and talked to the driver of Orvitz's bus. The driver wasn't sure that the man was Orvitz—he was wearing the disguise—but thought the man was he. The man did not get off the bus at any of the stops; Memphis was his destination. He looked at the ticket booths there and found that Orvitz and then bought a ticket to Chicago. He went to Chicago and found that the man then bought a ticket to Philadelphia. But no one remembered him. It was possible that the Philadelphia ticket was a ruse, and Bassoon set his sights on Chicago.

Bassoon worked with a slew of FBI agents. Some of them were sent to Philadelphia, but most of them fanned out and looked all over Chicago. They were dressed non-cryptically and casually looked everywhere. Each person had the picture of Orvitz and was looking for any kind of variation in it. They found nothing.

One day, when Bassoon was walking in the northern part of the city, he had a glimpse of a man rounding the corner a half-block away. His head was down. He looked like he was walking casually and had a slight limp. Bassoon kept his distance and was unenthusiastically following. No one saw him.

Bassoon had the man's apartment watched day and night. There was no movement from it. Then, after about a week, the man came out again, looking calm and dressed the same way. He was limping the same way, and it was impossible to tell if it was phony or real. Bassoon calmly walked toward him and when virtually up against him, stopped him and asked if he knew the president who was killed. The look in his eyes instantly gave him away. Bassoon arrested him and read him his rights, and, at long last, he had his man.

THE TRIAL

The entire FBI finally had Orvitz. They were ecstatic, but they were also cautious.

The man admitted that he was Orvitz, but that's all he gave. He claimed that he was an Arabian agent, that his group planned the whole attack, and that he would die for Allah if he had the chance. He was polite and spoke slowly. Silently, he knew that Ivanov would kill him if given half a chance. He hoped that that would never happen.

The American team was organized to try him, and this time, they had what they needed. His murder of Nell was golden. They had his fingerprints in the water sewer and the escape vehicle, and they had his collaboration with the Arabian terrorists who they captured. Nell's murder was solid. But they wanted his involvement in the killing of the president and the vice president as well, and they wanted that real bad. They were trying to assert a RICO claim against him, and they would stop at nothing to get it. Don't forget, they also had his photo with the two-dead assassins, and that made them very eager.

Bassoon was very cautious. He talked with Robinson and the whole team, and he repeatedly said that they had to be very careful. Among other things, he had a nagging doubt that an Arabian agent was all Orvitz was and a nagging doubt that someone else might try to kill him. They were unable to find any real background on him, and they couldn't be sure of his pedigree.

The trial was the biggest federal event ever. They told the public where he was kept, but there was no truth about it. He was kept in the most secure way that anyone ever was kept and always had at least three FBI agents with him. He had a stoic expression and never seemed to change it. His lawyer was appointed by the judge, from the criminal defense bar, and was commonly considered to be the best available choice. After all, there were not many lawyers who would take him.

Bassoon liked the story they would tell. The murder of Nell was in the bag, with the fingerprints and motive. The double murders of the president and vice president were more troubling. They seemed to have motive—that is they had a theory—but the only connection they had to them was through his getting out of the same car as both killers. The problem was the connection to the incredible room at the DC apartment, where Nell sent the bomb from, and who was responsible for giving them that information. That last point was the key. What country—it certainly was a country—had planned the whole thing and set them up with the key information was the whole ball game.

Bassoon had a theory that he told to anyone who'd listen. He didn't think that the Arabian connection was the key. It was too easy. And the Arabian agent who blurted out, "Praised be Allah," was too easy. He had a supposition who it was but absolutely no evidence. It could, of course, be anyone, and maybe it was, but he put his money on one country. Connecting Orvitz to the Russians was the holy grail, and he insisted that the absence of any connection to them was no accident.

They delved as deeply as they could into Orvitz's background. They knew he was part Indian and part Russian, but that was all they could establish, and Bassoon figured that that was no accident. He secretly wished they had some connection between Orvitz and the clandestine universe of Russian agents, but he figured that absence was no accident either.

They were to start with the story of how the two bombs were inserted into the ceremonies and by whom. They showed the two videos of the insertion of the two bombs and explained who the activists were. FBI agents, expert scientists, and procurers of work for the federal government, all told the story and emphasized that the timing of the two blasts was the key. Emphasizing the timing was crucial. A sophisticated entity planned the whole thing and thought it out from the beginning. Planting the remarkable two-bedroom apartment—carefully planned with the remarkable seventy-five-mile targeting capacity—was truly incredible and took months to set up, although they could not be sure who did it. An FBI agent familiar with the Russian set of agents in the United States gave it a quick review, just to suggest how it might have been handled. Finally, they tried to suggest motives for the terrible crimes, but objections were sustained, although the point was made.

Then they took the two bombers through the escape in the car to Poughkeepsie with the third, shadowy figure in the car. He was the ringleader. They told the story of the killing of Alright and Wassit, and they implied that all that was done by Orvitz in support of the plan. They also told the story of Nell, the great coup de grâce, and how it was brilliantly thwarted by the FBI and how Nell was captured red-handed with all the paraphernalia in place. There was a slight hint of who was responsible for all this planning, but no suggestion was made of who was responsible. Finally, they told the story of Nell's murder—which was surely the work of Orvitz—and how he had to try it twice to succeed. Here, they carefully told the story of how quickly one of the other agents implored Allah and made it seem so obvious that it might be a ploy.

It was a breathtaking and long story. Everyone had a place in it.

The chronology of the story was told by various FBI agents and was not disputed by anyone. Upon its completion, the government paused. Robinson looked happy, and, with a flourish, he rested.

The judge then turned toward the defendant's table and invited any defense case. They looked like he had something special to say and slowly announced, "I call Mr. Orvitz." The whole court let out a surprise, and the defense counsel had a grin. After a brief moment of shock, Mr. Ortiz took the stand.

Robinson was dumbfounded. It was absolutely the least expected move, and there was no way he was prepared. In fact, prepared for what? He had no idea.

Orvitz took the oath, looked like had something to say, and was seated.

Defense counsel asked his name and then said, "Do you have something to say, sir?"

"Yes, I do. I coordinated all the creative moves of this plan. It was a creative plan, of great skill and precision. The most inventive part was the seventy-five-mile section given to Nell, in great detail, putting Nell in charge of that part and then killing him. By far, that was the hardest. But the truth is, I was the origin of the plan. No country had a part in setting me in motion. It was all me. I contacted and arranged for Alright and Wassit. I ordered their execution. I ordered the failed plot to kill Nell and then the successful one. The agent you captured who said, 'Praise be to Allah,' and all his fellow actors were arranged by me. It was all me. It was my plan from top to bottom, and it worked perfectly. It was the greatest plan ever devised, and it will go down in history as the most famous, and infamous, plan ever attempted. You have caught me, that was not an accident, and I am here to say that I did it. That is my testimony."

"He's lying," said Robinson. "It's the biggest lie ever told. He's attempting to exonerate the country of origin and get them, whoever they are, off the hook. It won't work. It's absolutely impossible that he could have paid all the cost of doing that alone. It took millions of dollars. He's hiding that. We have to find it."

"Wait a minute," said Bassoon, "we don't have to find it. We just have to cross-examine. If it's impossible that he funded all that himself, we have to prove that on cross. Let's pulverize him."

"You're right," said Robinson. "Let's do it."

"So, Mr. Orvitz," Robinson said, rising to the challenge, "it was you who directed the placing of the American bomb that killed the president of the United States. Was it Wassit or Alright who placed it?"

"Wassit," said Orvitz. He had no expression. He expressed nothing.

"What did it cost you to pay Wassit to work in the job where she could do that?"

He drew a blank.

"I don't know," he said.

"Well, how long did she work in the job?" he asked.

"I don't know," he answered.

"Was it Wassit or Alright who placed the bomb that killed the vice president of the United States?"

"Alright."

"How long did he have to hold the job to do that task?"

"I don't know," he said.

"How did they get the jobs?"

"I don't know."

"You don't know," said Robinson, "well, who does?"

"I don't know."

"Mr. Orvitz, someone had to do that," said Robinson, "but you have no idea who?"

No answer.

"Mr. Orvitz, where did Ms. Wassit and Mr. Alright come from?"

"I don't know."

"Did you give orders to kill them both?"

"Yes."

"So you did not pay them. You do not know where they came from, but you killed them, is that right?"

"Yes."

"Mr. Orvitz, it sounds like you were their superiors in command but that you both were taking orders from someone else."

No answer.

He paused. This was a pretty good place to let it all sink in. He then continued.

"Mr. Orvitz, you all took orders from Russia, didn't you?"

"Objection," said the defense counsel. "There is no basis in the record for that."

"Sustained," said the judge.

"Mr. Orvitz, why did the fellows who tried to kill Nell refer to Allah?"

He paused. Then said, "Well, I think they were just trying to throw you off."

"Just trying to throw us off," said Robinson, "that's why they were so free in saying that?"

"Yes."

"So you must have come from somewhere else."

No answer.

"Your honor, could we have a short break?"

"Fifteen minutes," said the judge.

"That was terrific," said Bassoon. "It was great. You crucified him."

"Well, I think so. I think we got him to admit there's much he doesn't know. But who the hell does?"

"Russia," said Bassoon. "It has to be Russia."

"Yes," said Robinson. "It has to be."

"Okay," said Robinson. "What do we do?"

"I think we're done," said Bassoon. "Time to stop."

"Okay," said Robinson. "Period."

And so it was.

It was a strong cross-examination, and it was reviewed as such. The American team stopped there and delivered a guilty verdict in record time. The American team was given a strong welcome, and they thoroughly enjoyed it. But what would they do about Russia?

HISTORY

They all met with the secretary of state and then the president. The common thought was to blame Russia, but the problem was there was no proof. Different people had different ideas, and relations were never worse. Bilateral relations were about as bad as they could be, but they would have been worse if there was any proof. But what could they do?

Bassoon had an idea. "Why don't we try to get Ivanov to admit it?" he said. "Not publicly, but privately. We could then broadcast it to the whole world."

"That's idiocy," said Robinson. "We could never do that, could we?"

Bassoon said, "Well, why not? Suppose we got him to expose himself in front of the whole world. Sort of makes you feel vindicated."

"Yeah," said Robinson, "it does, but that doesn't make it any more real."

"Look," said Bassoon, "suppose it is possible. Wouldn't you want to try? Wouldn't you want to let him convict himself in front of the world?"

The silence was deafening. The group looked at each other.

"We'd have to get clearance from the very top," said Robinson.

"Yes, we would," said Bassoon, "and if we couldn't, that would be the end of it."

"Yes, it would," said Robinson, "and all hell would break loose."

"Let's ask," they all said.

And the greatest effort of all time proving that the evidence pointed to Russia was underway.

Evans talked to the director, who talked to the secretary of state, who talked to the president. Emotions were still extremely raw from the assassinations, and the president, who was still personally emotional from the assassinations, was ambivalent. But she—yes, it was a she—also wanted justice. After some soul-searching, she said the FBI could proceed cautiously and not make a big deal if it was unsuccessful. But, if it was successful, the FBI could shout it from the treetops and have the most compelling case of espionage in the world.

Bassoon, Robinson, and the entire team met with Evans and the director. They talked at great length. It seemed no one had a good way to try. They considered it at great length, and then Bassoon said, "Well, why don't we try to arrange it to make Ivanov speak privately to a trusted ally and have him admit it. It won't be easy, and the trick is that if it doesn't work, nothing is lost. But if it works, we'll have the greatest admission in history."

Silence.

Then Evans said, "It's a long shot, but if it doesn't work, no harm, no foul. If it does, it surely was worth it."

"Well, how would we try it?" asked Robinson. "To whom would Ivanov be willing to admit it?"

"That's the hardest part," said Bassoon. "We couldn't use an FBI agent, and we couldn't use someone we could trust. We'd have to find someone that *he* trusts explicitly and have a way to get him out of there right after it's done. It's very risky."

"Well," said Evans, "it has to be someone that we could trust posing it to, in case it doesn't work out, and be sure it doesn't get back to Ivanov. Does such a person exist?"

No one had an answer. They all promised to think about it. The hardest part was, assuming he could trust the person, helping the person get so close to Ivanov that he could trust him or her.

None of America's best secret agents would do the trick. Neither would anyone that Ivanov didn't know. It had to be someone whom Ivanov knew well, who would be willing to do it. And it was suicide to ask somebody without knowing the answer.

Well, there were lots of people who knew Ivanov fairly well, but none could be asked. Someone had to be found who knew him well who could be asked. That seemed impossible.

Bassoon had an idea. "Why don't you place a very secret agent in the middle of his group, and let him get to know people? After a while, he could possibly find someone. If not, there's no harm."

"That's possible," said Evans. "Seems like a long shot, but it might work. If not, then nothing is lost. Let's think about who we could use that way."

Bassoon knew someone who might be a place to start. He was a European, a German agent, and had the personality they wanted. His name was Friedrick and would be willing to talk. So Bassoon met with him and talked privately.

"You know," said Bassoon, "we have an idea. It comes from the terrible assassinations we recently had. We were wondering if there was someone we could trust who could, in speaking to Ivanov, get him to admit that it was his doing. He would have a very secret wire—so it could never be found—and we would get the admission on tape. It would be the greatest admission ever made. The one who gets it would get the hell out of there and be remembered as a hero. It would probably be the end of Ivanov."

"Jesus," said Friedrick, "that's crazy. If it doesn't work, the poor man would be a goner. You'd have to find someone you could trust absolutely, who knows Ivanov well, and who wouldn't mind undoing him. Where would you find such a man?"

"Well," said Bassoon, "I don't know. I surely don't have anyone in mind. Our guy would have to have an eye out for someone and not be afraid to raise the subject. It's a tall order. And if it doesn't work, at least the two men are goners."

"And if it does work, the Russian agent would be a hero," said Friedrick.

"Think about it," said Bassoon, "and let me know how you feel about it. If you never want to hear about it again, just let me know. If you do, let's talk about it further."

"Okay," said Friedrick.

Bassoon knew what Friedrick would say. But the hardest part would be finding someone. There still might be no one who could do it.

About a month later, Friedrick got in touch with Bassoon. They met alone. Friedrick said, "There's someone who might do it. I've known him for a while, and he's fed up with the Russian style but afraid to say anything. He's personally extremely mad at Ivanov, over a hazy personal matter, but no one in the Russian apparatchik knows about it. He's a mid-level member of the Politburo, with ties to the secret police. His name is Vladimer. I obviously have said nothing to him."

Bassoon was silent for a long while. Then said, "Wow, he sounds perfect. Does he have family who would be in danger?"

"Yes," said Friedrick.

"But his relatives might be left unharmed once the cat is out of the bag," said Bassoon.

"That's true," said Friedrick, "but the problem is that we won't know for sure until it's right upon us. There isn't a way to know for sure."

"That's true," said Bassoon.

Bassoon briefed the whole thing to Evans. Evans was cool on the subject. "It's much too risky," he said, "and there's no way to be sure dozens of ways don't go south. We can't afford to try it."

"True," said Bassoon, "but think about what could really go bad if it doesn't work."

"It could be fatal to the guy who would try," said Evans, "and we'd have hell to pay for making the effort."

"Well," said Bassoon, "not really. Ivanov would never really make it public if it didn't work."

"I guess that's right," said Evans. "Let me talk to people above me."

After a while, Evans returned and said, "Guess what, they want to give it a try. There's an incredible amount of anger over the assassinations. When the time comes, they will do everything possible to protect the innocent parties."

"Good," said Bassoon. "Let's give it a try."

Bassoon sat down with Friedrick. The ground rules were clear and could not be broken. Friedrick fully understood and was ecstatic to help. He had already been checked out by the highest possible authorities, and they were clear that they were in the best possible hands. In fact, unbeknownst to anyone, the president had privately cleared it with the chancellor of Germany.

"So, Friedrick," said Bassoon, "we have clearance. You can be careful and privately raise it with Vladimer. You must tell him that he can say no if he wants and take his time to think about too. It's up to you, but you can also tell him that, if he agrees to do it, he will have the full protection of the president of the United States."

"Good," said Friedrick. "I'll need to take my time in talking to him. I might be able to do it at the meeting that's scheduled for next month in Paris, but I can't promise anything."

"I know," said Bassoon, "and I wouldn't want to rush you."

"I'll keep you posted," said Friedrick. And that was it.

Bassoon waited a month and then some. One day, when he least expected it, he bumped into Friedrick, and he knew it wasn't an accident.

"All done," said Friedrick. "He was very willing. Our conversation was totally private, and he didn't have to think about for very long. He asked in passing if he'd have protection for his family, and I told him that he absolutely would. He said he'll do it, but it might take some time. He has to arrange for it at the right time, and it might never happen, but he'll look for the chance. And I told him all about the special recorder that you gave me, how it works, and he practiced it many times. I think we are all ready. We just have to wait."

"That's great," said Bassoon. "We'll wait."

He also passed the preparation up the food chain.

Vladimer was very cautious. He was an acceptable, likable young man, with two kids and a wife, each with relatively large families. He was up and coming, with a star on, but with a very private beef and a very private grudge. Known to only a few people, one of his great-grandfathers was a Jew, who lived under an eternal threat of persecution that he never talked about. Luckily, his name was hidden, and almost no one knew about it, but to Vladimer, his story was very painful. He wanted Ivanov to know—he did not—and he wanted his family to be treated right. It was a very private matter.

Vladimer worked in circles where he sometimes came into contact with Ivanov, but not frequently and not for too long. He was gregarious and funny and universally well-liked. He treated Ivanov with great deference, would have given his life for him. That was the way to get ahead.

One day, he was in a meeting and on a break, found himself briefly alone with Ivanov. He said something hilariously funny and found Ivanov laughing with him. Ivanov asked him something funny, he laughed and kept his space. Then he had the chance, and he took it. With less laughter, but still in a good mood, he said something less funny, but still acceptably Russian. Without beating a lash, Ivanov said, "Oh, I never was so happy. I had the president and vice president assassinated, and it was the greatest thrill of my life. I felt like I was king of the world."

When he stopped, two other people returned, and he regained his composure. Actually, he didn't have to regain any composure, he privately winked at Vladimer, and he never knew what happened. He did not know he had made the greatest admission of all time.

The admission was clearly on tape, and the United States had it. They kept it quiet and allowed Vladimer to continue his ruse and then to calmly move all his fairly large family out of Russia, to Germany, and then to the United States. When he was in the clear, and already renamed with special names, the American President went on air and played the tape for all the world. She did it with all the gusto she could muster, and all the world heard, "Oh, I never was so happy. I had the president and vice president assassinated, and it was the greatest thrill of my life. I felt like I was king of the world."

All the world heard his voice, and there was no difficulty in saying it was his. The reaction was unbelievable. The reaction was swift, unanimous, and devastating. He tried to weather it, but he couldn't. Suddenly, in a remarkably quick move, he was removed from office, put under arrest, and another younger personal officer took his place. It was bloodless and definitive. And so, the reign of Ivanov was over.

The entire American hierarchy was ecstatic. It was a great reminder of what the United States of America was all about.

Bassoon, Friedrick, and Evans met for a time, and the three of them were summoned to the White House, where they finally met Vladimer. It was a sad and a wonderful meeting.

EPILOGUE

The president of the United States said the following, in a speech to the nation and the world:

"Ladies and gentlemen, our nation is today still in mourning but is still moving on. With the murderous killing of our two elected officials, and the treacherous killer in justice in his own country, the world is a better place. But I want to say something. When it is time to run for president next year, I will not run. I would not have had the awesome power of this office had not the greatest crime in the history of mankind been created. I will not take it as an advantage. The wisdom of our country is in limiting the length of our office to four years. Four little years is a precious small time. If the tenure is good, the officeholder is entitled to only four more. Nothing more. There is then an election, in all fifty states and the American Virgin Islands, and for four more years, our nation is the envy of the world. And it goes on. Next year, the rebirth of our nation will go on, as it will until mankind roams the earth no more. Our rebirth continues, and so may it always. God bless the United States of America."

Bassoon went back to his wife and his family. His kids jumped all over him, and his wife was giddy. He sat and looked out the window and thought about all the places he had been to. The next day, he went to work.

The End

ABOUT THE AUTHOR

Frederick S. Gold practiced law for almost forty years. He ran a trial practice course for the Connecticut Bar Association and taught a class at Yale Law School for many years. During his fortieth year as a lawyer, he had a debilitating stroke and was no longer able to practice law. He then wrote this book as a labor of love.